THE DODOS DID IT!

ALM

For my sisters,
Elner and Frankie

Also by Alice McKinley:
NINE LIVES
NEWTON

FRANKIE

SIMON & SCHUSTER

First published in Great Britain in 2021 by Simon & Schuster UK Ltd
1st Floor, 222 Gray's Inn Road, London, WC1X 8HB

A CIP catalogue record for this book is available from the British Library upon request

ISBN: 978-1-4711-8122-1 (HB) • ISBN: 978-1-4711-8121-4 (PB) • ISBN: 978-1-4711-8123-8 (eBook)

Printed in China • 10 9 8 7 6 5 4 3 2 1

THE DODOS DID IT!

AMY

BRUCE

EGGY

HELEN

JANE

MILO

ELNER

SCUBIE

MARIO

ALICE McKINLEY

SIMON & SCHUSTER
London New York Sydney Toronto New Delhi

Jack didn't just like dodos.
He **LOVED** them.

He owned dodo toys,
watched dodo films,

and even had
dodo lampshades.

But what he wanted the most,
more than ANYTHING in the world,
was his very own pet dodo.

"I wish,
I wish,
I WISH
I had a dodo!"
said Jack.

Little did he know,
his wish was about to come . . .

"I can't believe it!" said Jack.
"My very own dodo – at last!"

Jack was having
so much fun,
he wished for
even more dodos.

And he got more . . .

and more . . .

. . . and MORE!

At first it was the best thing ever . . .

but before too long,
Jack realised
that ten pet dodos

were a little more trouble
than he thought
they'd be.

Mum and Dad were NOT happy
when they saw the mess.

"BUT IT WASN'T ME!" cried Jack.

"The dodos did it!"

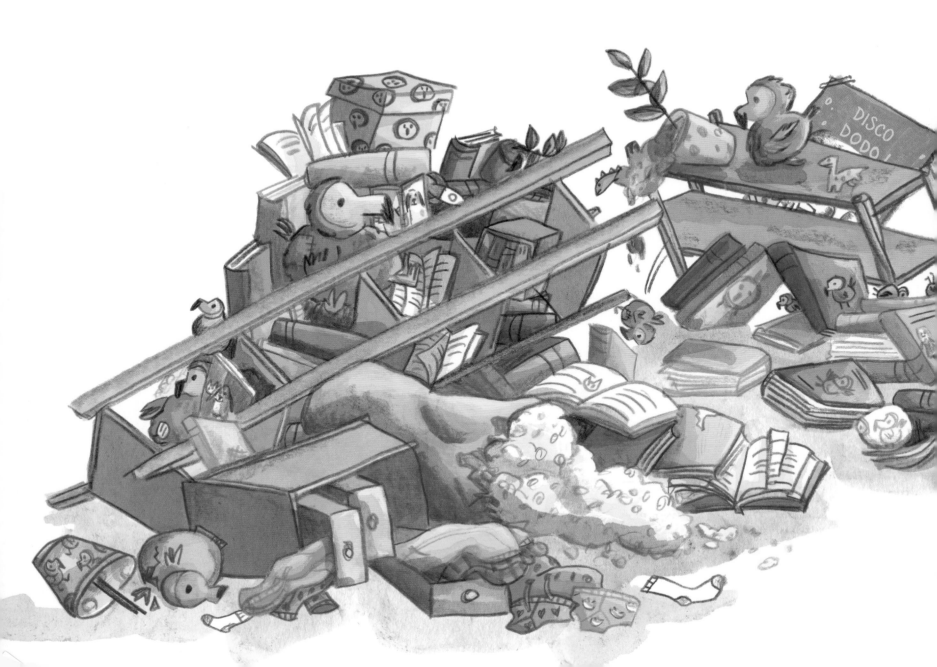

"Don't be silly, Jack – dodos are extinct!" said Dad.

"Come on, we'll be late for your swimming lesson."

But Jack couldn't escape the dodos at the swimming pool.

They were diving and splashing and having a lovely time!

Things were bad at the playground . . .

"It wasn't me!
The dodos did it!"

And as for the supermarket, well . . .

"The dodos did it!"

It just.
Wasn't.
FAIR.

"I wish all these dodos would disappear and I only had one pet!" said Jack.

Little did Jack know,
his wish was about
to come . . .

AAARRRRR!"

"Uh-oh. You really SHOULD be careful
what you wish for!" said Jack.

The noise from Jack's new pet brought his parents up the stairs.

"Jack, what's all that racket? You'll disturb the neighbours!" shouted Dad.

"Let me guess," said Mum.
"The dodos did it?"

"Actually . . ." said Jack.

"It was my new pet dinosaur!"